Good Night, Gorilla

Peggy Rathmann

MAMMOTH

874

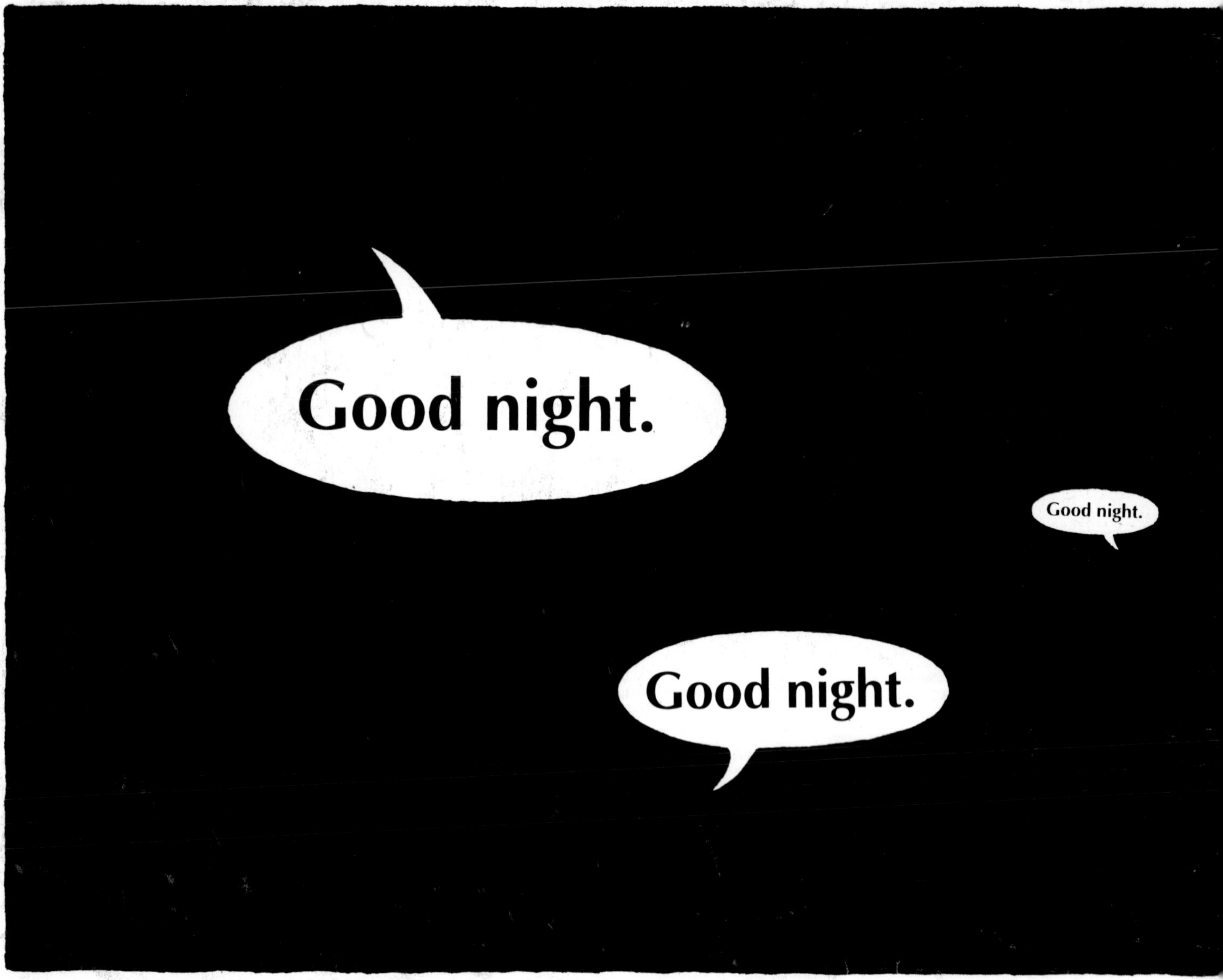
Good night.
Good night.
Good night.

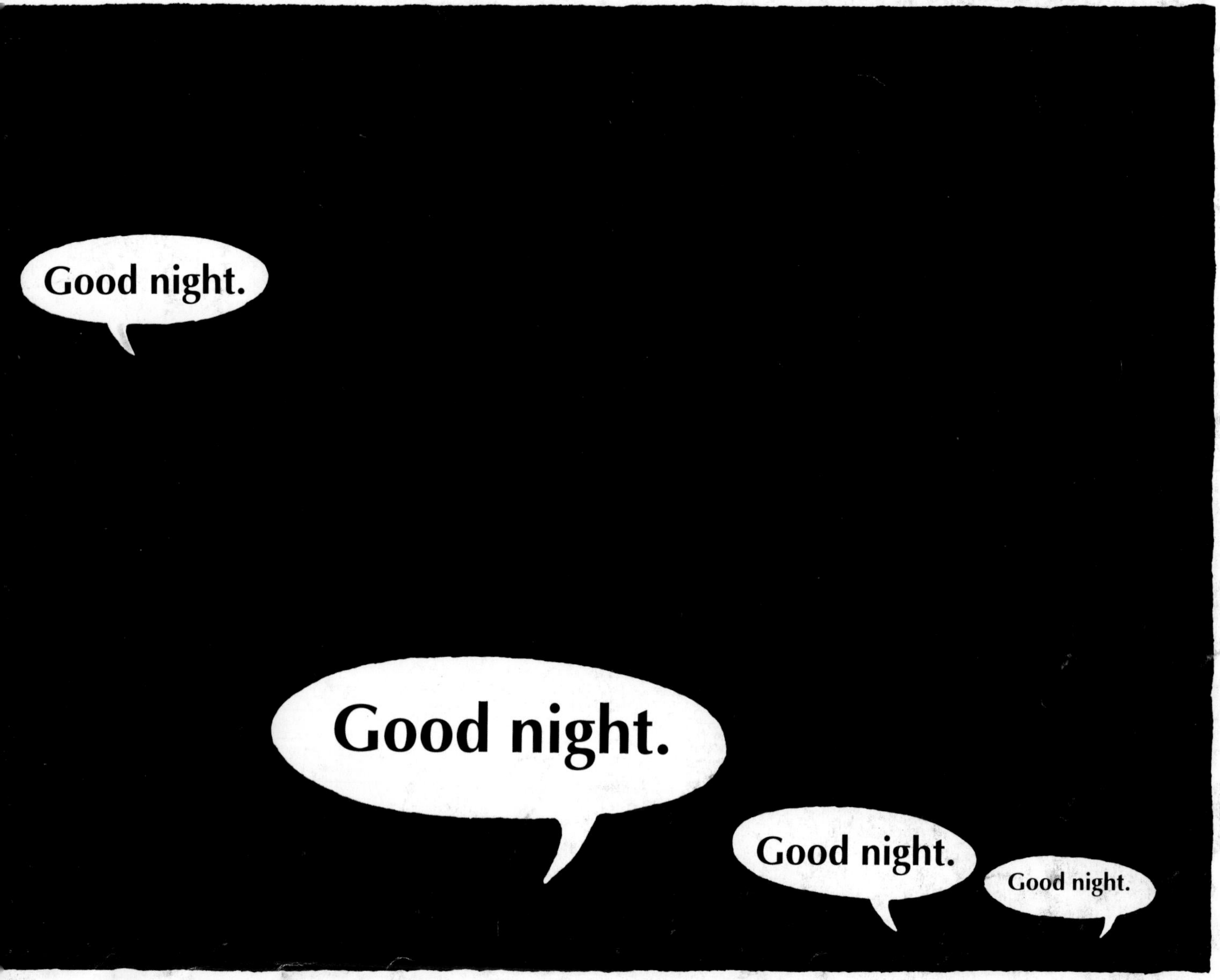
Good night.
Good night.
Good night.
Good night.

**For Mr. and Mrs. Joseph McQuaid,
and all their little gorillas**

First published in Great Britain 1994
by William Heinemann Ltd
Published 1995 by Mammoth
an imprint of Reed Consumer Books Ltd
Michelin House, 81 Fulham Road, London SW3 6RB
and Auckland, Melbourne, Singapore and Toronto

Text and illustrations copyright © Peggy Rathmann 1994

Reprinted 1995 (twice)
ISBN 0 7497 2312 2

A CIP catalogue record for this title
is available from the British Library

Produced by Mandarin Offset
Printed and bound in Hong Kong